Robert Chambers

Edinburgh Papers; Edinburgh Merchants and Merchandise in Old Times, Lecture

in large print

MEGALI

Robert Chambers

Edinburgh Papers; Edinburgh Merchants and Merchandise in Old Times, Lecture

in large print

Reproduction of the original.

1st Edition 2023 | ISBN: 978-3-38708-162-6

Megali Verlag is an imprint of Outlook Verlagsgesellschaft mbH.

Verlag (Publisher): Outlook Verlag GmbH, Zeilweg 44, 60439 Frankfurt, Deutschland
Vertretungsberechtigt (Authorized to represent): E. Roepke, Zeilweg 44, 60439 Frankfurt, Deutschland
Druck (Print): Books on Demand GmbH, In de Tarpen 42, 22848 Norderstedt, Deutschland

EDINBURGH PAPERS

EDINBURGH MERCHANTS
AND
MERCHANDISE IN OLD TIMES

BY

ROBERT CHAMBERS, F.R.S.E.,

1859.

TO THE
MERCHANT COMPANY OF EDINBURGH,
THIS LECTURE, DELIVERED AT THEIR REQUEST,
FEBRUARY 14, 1859,
IS RESPECTFULLY INSCRIBED.

EDINBURGH MERCHANTS AND
MERCHANDISE IN OLD TIMES.

I DO not propose, on this occasion, to carry your minds back to a very remote period, for, truth to tell, Scotland was not distinguished for commerce at an early date. You will not be surprised if I briefly remark that we hear nothing of trade in Leith harbour till the reign of Bruce, and have reason to believe that it hardly had an existence for a century later. Dr Nicolas West, an emissary of Henry VIII., visited Scotland in 1513, just before the battle of Flodden, and he tells us that he then found at Leith only nine or ten small topmen, or ships with rigging, which, from his remarks, we may infer to have all been under sixty tons burden. There was then but a meagre traffic carried on with the Low Countries, France, and Spain—wool, skins, and salmon carried out; and wine, silks, cloth, and miscellaneous articles imported: matters altogether so insignificant, that there are but a few scattered references to them in the acts of the national parliament. One may have some idea of the pettiness of any external trade carried on by Edinburgh in the early part of the sixteenth century, from what we know of the condition of Leith at that time. It was but a village, without quay or pier, and with no approach to the harbour except by an alley—the still existing Burgess Close, which in some parts is not above four feet wide. We must imagine any merchandise then brought to Leith as carried in vessels of the size of small yachts, and borne off to the Edinburgh warehouses slung on horseback, through the narrow defiles of the Burgess Close.

It chances that we possess, in our General Register House, a very distinct memorial of the traffic carried on between Scotland and the Netherlands at the close of the fifteenth century. It consists in the ledger of Andrew Halyburton, a Scottish merchant conducting commission business for his countrymen at Middleburg, and conservator of the Scotch privileges there. It extends from the year 1493 to 1505. Andrew acted as agent for a number of eminent persons, churchmen as well as laymen, besides merchants, receiving and selling for a commission the raw products of the country, chiefly those just named—wool, hides, and salmon—and sending home in return nearly every kind of manufactured article which we could suppose to have then been in use. It appears that even salt was then imported. Wheel-barrows were sent from Flanders to assist in building King's College, Aberdeen. There were cloths of silk, linen, and woollen; fruits, spiceries, and drugs; plate and jewellery; four kinds of wine—claret, Gascony claret, Rhenish, and Malvoisie. Paper is often named; and there is mention of pestles and mortars, basins of brass, chamber-mats, beds of arras, feather-beds, down-pillows, vermilion, red and white lead, and pins. John of Pennycuik imports the image of Thomas-à-Becket, bought from a painter at Antwerp. More than one tombstone is shipped to a Scotch order from Middleburg. Once there is a 'kist of buikis' for a physician at Aberdeen. The account between Halyburton and the Abbot of Holyrood may be cited as an example of its class in this curious tome. For 'my lord,' as Halyburton calls him, he sells the wool of the sheep which ranged the Abbey's pastures in Tweeddale, and the skins and hides of the sheep and cattle which were slaughtered for the table at Holyrood. He buys in return claret and other wines, apples, olives, oranges, figs, raisins, almonds, rice, loaf-sugar, ginger, mace, pepper, saffron, and large quantities of apothecaries' wares. Amongst other customers, we find Walter Chapman, the first printer in Scotland, and John Smollett, the ancestor of the great novelist of the last century. Halyburton appears to have often visited Edinburgh, settling old accounts, and arranging new ventures. Each account has the name of 'JHESUS' piously superscribed; and where the customer was a trader, the merchant's *mark*, which was cut upon his boxes or inscribed upon his bales, is copied into the ledger. The volume is surprisingly like a ledger of the present day, even in the particular of binding; but it gives, on the whole, the idea of a poor and narrow range of traffic—the traffic of a rude country, producing only raw articles, and few of them, and dependent for all above the simplest which it consumed, upon foreign states.[1]

About the time referred to in this volume, the central line of street between the West Bow and Nether Bow was the chief place of merchandise in Edinburgh, the Cowgate and Canongate being more specially the residence of the nobility, gentry, and great ecclesiastics. There were two chief classes of goods dealt in, each mainly confined to a particular section of the street. What was called *Inland Merchandise*, or *Inland'sh Goods*—namely, yarn, stockings, coarse cloth, and other such articles made at home—were, by a charter of 1477, ordained to be sold in the upper part of the street, then without a special name, but which is subsequently referred to as the *Land-market*—apparently an abbreviation of *Inland Market*, from the description of goods sold in it. Down to recent times, such goods continued to be chiefly sold there, by people occupying *laigh shops*, and on a certain day exposing their wares by ancient privilege on the open street. The remainder of the High Street was chiefly devoted to a superior class of traders, calling themselves *Merchants*, dealers in imported wares of various kinds, and each occupying a booth or shop, besides whatever other warehouses in more retired situations. Wholesale and retail dealers alike passed under this name, as is still, indeed, the case to a considerable extent in Scotland, where it has always been remarked that there was a peculiar liberality or courtesy in the distribution of names and titles. We frequently hear in the journalists and chroniclers of the old time, of the *Merchants Buithes*, or shops. The only other kind of shops in those days was the kind called *krames*, generally very small, made out of mere angles of property, or insinuated between the buttresses of St Giles's Kirk, and chiefly devoted to the sale of toys and other petty articles. We often hear of *krames*, of *kramers* (that is, krame-keepers), and *kramery* (that is, small wares sold in krames) in the familiar histories of that age, and in old titles. Dunbar, the early Scottish poet, describes these shops very aptly as

'Hampered in ane honey-kaim,'

close to St Giles's Church. Fixing our attention, meanwhile, on the class of traders called merchants, we find that their booths were in general small places, situated behind the open arcade which then ran along the greater part of the High Street on both sides. The whole front of one of these booths, consisting of folding boards, was opened by day—one board being drawn up, another let down, one or more folded back sideways, so as to display the interior to the passer-by. On a bench or counter within the front-wall, goods were laid out to attract attention; in some instances, there were also stands set out for the display of wares under the shelter of the arcade in front. As the merchant sat in his open booth, there were sights presented to him different from what he would now see: amongst others, rival nobles meeting on the causey, with their respective bands of armed followers, and fighting out their quarrels with sword and buckler, and the more deadly hagbut, to quell which our traders were enjoined by civic statute of 1529, to keep each in his booth 'ane axe, or twa, or three, after as they have servants,' and to be ready to use them. If we are to believe Dunbar, he saw 'the gait' filthy, and full of clamorous beggars, milk, shell-fish, and puddings sold at the Cross and the Tron, and vile crafts everywhere more prominent than his own respectable merchandise. In the town of Berne, in Switzerland, you can see precisely the same structural arrangements still existing along both sides of the principal street, which further reminds one of ancient Edinburgh by its name of *Kramgasse*.

At length, in the progress of improvement, there were some shops formed in a certain part of the High Street, having those open arcaded spaces in front closed up, leaving only a window and a door; and these places of business, by way of distinction, acquired the name of *luckenbooths*—that is, closed booths, a term, as you are all aware, which still gives a name to the portion of street referred to. Berne is now in exactly the same circumstances in this respect as Edinburgh was two hundred years ago, for there also we find a few shops of more ambitious character than their neighbours, with the fronts built up. It is very interesting thus to trace in continental towns of the present day a reflex of things long ago prevalent in our own city. I was amused, at Nuremberg, to find the Frauenkirke barnacled all round with little shops or *krames*, as I remember St Giles's to have been, each petty shop, moreover, having its miniature house above, in one or more stories, affording a stifling accommodation to the traders, as was the case with several of the krame-shops of the old Parliament Close.

In Germany and Scandinavia, we still find traders who, while conducting a considerable wholesale business, and even a little banking, have also retail shops, generally placed towards the public street, and conducted by subalterns. I found such men in Iceland attending the parties given in the governor's house, and evidently enjoying the local consideration due to their wealth and education. In Edinburgh, in the sixteenth and seventeenth centuries, there were traffickers of this kind, some planted in the great thoroughfares, and some in more retired situations. They were, in some instances, men with pretensions to pedigree—men who took a prominent part in public affairs, entertained princes and sovereigns, founded families, and so forth. Thus, a Hamilton of the house of Innerwick, was what was called a *merchant* in the West Bow; he acquired lands—he fell as a gallant gentleman in Pinkie field; his eldest son was the ancestor of the Earls of Haddington; his second son, a secular priest, was rector of the University of Paris, and one of the council of the League who offered the French crown to the king of Spain in 1591. Contemporary with him, occupying a shop in the middle row of buildings alongside of St Giles's Church, was a similar merchant, named Edward Hope; his father is believed to have been a Frenchman who came to Scotland in the train of the Princess Magdalen, daughter of Francis I., when she was wedded to James V. in 1537. While externally but a shopkeeper in the Luckenbooths, there can be no doubt that Edward Hope carried on foreign trade upon a considerable scale, and was a man of large means; of which last fact, his extensive mansion in Tod's Close, Castlehill, stood a few years ago as good evidence. This worthy merchant was commissioner for Edinburgh in the parliament which settled the Reformation, and he afterwards, for Protestantism's sake, bore the brunt of the Lady Mary's gentle wrath. Through his elder son he was the ancestor of all the Hopes who have since stood so conspicuous in rank, in wealth, and in public service in Scotland; while from his younger son are descended the famous mercantile family of the Hopes of Amsterdam. In the latter part of the sixteenth century—that is, in the reigns of Mary and James VI.—notwithstanding the constant civil broils, and the false maxims by which commerce was to appearance protected or favoured, but in reality depressed—there appear to have been some considerable merchants in Edinburgh, and merchants really entitled to the name, being conductors of foreign traffic and dealers in wholesale. They generally had their establishments in some comparatively retired situation, in a close or *wynd*, near the centre of the city. In Riddell's Close, Lawnmarket, there still exist the mansion and business premises of one of these considerable merchants, namely, Bailie John Macmoran. We are told by the church historian, Calderwood, that he was the greatest merchant of his day in Edinburgh, but disliked by the clergy, because of his carrying victual to Spain, thus endangering the souls of the Scottish mariners by contact with popery. His house is a good and not inelegant building forming a court, the entrance to which still exhibits the hooks for the massive gates by which it could be closed up at night and in times of danger. A stone projection over a window indicates an arrangement for pulleying up goods into an upper chamber. A large room or hall in which the queen's brother, the Duke of Holstein, was entertained 'with great solemnity and merriness' in 1597, shews the wealthy state in which this merchant lived. John, who had been a servitor or dependent of the Regent Morton, whose treasures he assisted to conceal, was cut off in the middle of his prosperous career, by a pistol bullet fired at him by a High School boy, while he was exerting his authority as a magistrate in suppressing a barring-out.

Near to Macmoran's house, in what was latterly called the Old Bank Close, there stood till our own time the not less handsome establishment of a merchant named Robert Gourlay, bearing the date 1569. This was a large and, in some respects, elegant building, such as could not be constructed in our day for less than two thousand five hundred pounds. It had a ground-floor directly accessible from the close, and which we may presume to have been a store for unbroken bales and packages; then a first floor, which was probably the warehouse for wholesale and retail traffic—this had a stair-entrance for itself; next there was a second floor, accessible by its own stair likewise, and from which there was an inner stair enclosed in a hanging turret, giving access to two upper floors; these last three floors constituting the accommodation of the merchant's family. We find that Gourlay, who had originally been a dependent of the Duke of Chastelherault, carried on a large business in the exporting of corn, doubtless importing in return the many various articles which he distributed from his first floor. It is to be feared that he and some of his contemporaries occasionally were indebted for large profits to favour purchased from the bad and ignorant governments of their day. At least, we find that Robert, in 1574, bought a licence from the Regent Morton, enabling him to export grain, while, owing to a dearth, this power was denied to all others. The kirk, which he served as an elder, challenged him for this inhumane traffic, and he for some time stood out under the Regent's protection, but was at last obliged to succumb, and make public confession of his offence, standing in the *marriage-place* in St Giles's, clad in a gown made on purpose, and which he had to bestow thereafter on the poor. Robert lived to accommodate his friend the Regent, in his house, for two or three days, when the latter was awaiting the stroke of the Maiden under a hired guard; and a few years later, when King James deemed Holyrood an unsafe residence, by reason that the Earl of Bothwell was scouring about in quest of him, he had up-putting for several days in the house of the rich merchant, Robert Gourlay.

I may enumerate a few other considerable merchants of this period, all of whom had good houses in the city, where they dwelt as well as carried on business. In what was latterly called Brodie's Close, between Macmoran's and

Gourlay's houses, lived William Little of Over-Libberton, at one time provost, and the ancestor of the family now represented by Mr Little Gilmour of the Inch. It connects merchandise in an interesting manner with professional and literary things, that Clement, the brother of William, was the commissary of Edinburgh, and one of the greatest benefactors to the infant university. Provost Little's house, dated 1570, was taken down so lately as 1836, having continued all the time an entailed property of the family. The *North British Advertiser* printing-office now stands on its site. Nicol Udwart, an active and wealthy merchant, had a stately house surrounding a square court in Niddry's Wynd; and there King James was living in February 1591, when the Bonny Earl of Moray was slaughtered at Dunnibrissle. A neighbour of Udwart, styled Alexander Clark of Balbirnie, also a wealthy merchant, and at one time provost of the city, gave accommodation at the same time to the Chancellor Maitland. On another occasion, a little earlier, we hear of King James living with William Fowler, who was also a merchant in Edinburgh. The king, it is stated, went out to hunt, promising to return to dinner in Fowler's house at *one o'clock*. Fowler lived in the Anchor Close, and his house, in which, as we see, he had entertained royalty, was taken down only three months ago by the Railway Access Company. It stood, indeed, in a narrow alley; but it had the advantage of a free aspect over the country to the north of the city. In the index to the state-papers connected with Scotland, lately published by Mr Thorpe, William Fowler figures as a partisan of the English protestant interest, continually engaged in giving information to Sir Francis Walsingham.

The trades of Edinburgh in those days were generally conducted by men of small account; but there was one art carried on upon a scale which raised its practitioners to the grade of merchants. This was the craft of the goldsmiths. The habits of the upper classes, partaking so much of an ill-supported ostentation, made this comparatively a great trade. We have all heard much of George Heriot, who was made goldsmith to the queen in 1597, and who, afterwards transplanting himself to London, there completed the fortune which became the means of founding his celebrated hospital. But there was a contemporary Edinburgh goldsmith of even greater importance, in the person of Thomas Foulis, who seems to have been to King James what the Bank of England was to William Pitt two hundred years later. It was a loan from Thomas which enabled the king to march against the rebellious Catholic lords at Aberdeen in 1593. He stood creditor to the king, in the ensuing year, for the sum of £14,598 Scots, and for this James lodged with him two gold drinking-cups, amounting in all to the weight of fifteen pounds five ounces. In May 1601, the royal debt to

Thomas amounted to the enormous sum of £180,000 Scots, and a parliamentary arrangement had to be made for its payment. One of the benefits which Thomas Foulis derived from being the king's creditor to so large an amount, was a grant of the lead-mines of Lanarkshire, which he worked with good result, and handed ultimately to his granddaughter, who married James Hope, the ancestor of the noble family of Hopetoun. Thus, it will be observed, what constituted, and yet in part constitutes, the fortune of the Earls of Hopetoun, came originally from one of our Parliament Close goldsmiths.

The relation of the last resident king of Scots to his mercantile subjects in Edinburgh was generally a good-humoured one; but there was one occasion when serious strife stood between them, though for a short time only. Under some misapprehension about his intentions regarding the clergy, a mob beset his majesty for an hour or two in the place of judgment in the Tolbooth. He was, or affected to be, very wroth with the people of Edinburgh, and returning on Hogmanay day, a fortnight after the riot, he ordered that the ports and streets should be kept for his protection by certain Border chiefs on whom he could depend. A rumour arose that *Kinmont Willie* and other border thieves were come to *spulyie* the town, and immediately there was such a scene as no Edinburgh merchant then living could ever forget. The principal men took the goods out of their booths, and transported them to the strongest house in the town—possibly Macmoran's—posting themselves and servants there also, all fully armed, in apprehension of an immediate attack. In like manner, groups of the craftsmen and commoner sort of people gathered into strong houses, with their best goods, and with arms in their hands to defend their property to the last extremity. An Edinburgh citizen, John Birrel, chronicles this affair, with the remark—'Judge, gentle reader, gif this be play.' After all, the guard of borderers did our merchants and craftsmen no harm; but when one reads of such an alarm, it becomes easy to understand how Macmoran and Gourlay had such strong houses for conducting their business, and how all the closes in the High Street should have had gates at top and bottom, as still appears in many cases by the remaining hooks for the hinges.

When we pass on to the early part of the seventeenth century, we still find merchants of considerable importance in Edinburgh. They usually are either the descendants or the progenitors of good families. As an example of the former, we may take James Murray, of whose living locality in our city I can say nothing, but who, at his death in old age in 1649, was laid in the Greyfriars' Churchyard. James was a younger son of Patrick Murray of Philiphaugh, and to each of his three sons, by Bethia Maule of the Panmure family, he left an estate. Perhaps I could in no way better describe him than by the quaint words of his epitaph in the Greyfriars:

Stay, passenger, and shed a tear,
For good James Murray lieth here;
He was of Philiphaugh descended,
And for his merchandise commended;
He was a man of a good life,
Married Bethia Maule to 's wife;
He may thank God that e'er he gat her;
She bore him three sons and a daughter;
The first he was a man of might,
For which the king made him a knight;
The second was both wise and wily,
For which the town made him a bailie;
The third, a factor of renown,
Both in Campvere and in this town.
His daughter was both grave and wise,
And married was to James Elies.

Another of this class was John Trotter, son of Thomas Trotter of Catchelraw. He acquired by merchandise in Edinburgh the means of purchasing the estate of Mortonhall, and thus laid the foundation of a family which still exists in great note and opulence. A third was John Sinclair, a cadet of the old house of Longformacus. Being bred a merchant, as Douglas's *Baronage* explicitly declares, he realised so much wealth by his business as to be able, in 1624, to purchase the estate of Stevenston in Haddingtonshire, to which he afterwards added other lands, forming in whole a large estate. The king conferred on him a Nova Scotia baronetcy, which is still enjoyed by his descendants. We have a fourth instance in George Blair, a second son of Patrick Blair of Pittendreich. The wealth which this gentleman acquired by merchandise in Edinburgh, was the means of purchasing the estate of Lethendy in Perthshire, to which his son added that of Glasclune. Another may still be added, in James Riddell, of the ancient family of Riddell of that Ilk. This gentleman, after pursuing a business career for some time in Poland, where many Scotch youths then found occupation, returned to Edinburgh about the year 1603, set up business there, married a lady of means styled Bessie Allan, and died a wealthy man. His son, who became a merchant in Leith, purchased the estate of Kinglass, which he left to a line of descendants. I cannot but view with interest the good sense of our gentry of two and three hundred years ago, in setting their younger sons to a career of useful and honourable industry, instead of allowing them idly to loiter at home, or go into the little better than idleness of a foreign military service. It was evidently considered no discredit in those days for a gentleman's son to become a merchant in Edinburgh.

In the age which we now have under our notice, the proceedings of mercantile men were impeded and thwarted, to a degree of which we can scarcely form an idea, by false political economy. For a merchant to reserve grain during a scarcity—thus, in the view of Adam Smith, serving a good public end by equalising consumption over the distressed period—was then an impious crime condemned by whole legions of laws. To export almost any article that could be consumed at home was generally discountenanced, as tending to raise prices upon the home consumer. Importing foreign articles was looked upon at the best as a lamentable necessity, because it caused money to be sent out of the country. We have, for instance, in 1615, a fulmination from the Privy Council against a 'most unlawful and pernicious tred of exporting eggs furth of the kingdom,' and in 1625, a not less furious denunciation of the 'mischeant and wicked tred' of exporting tallow. In 1634, a man wanting some Norway timber to build houses at Seaton, required to use influence with the government to be allowed to send some of his own East Lothian wheat for it to Bergen. An unenlightened selfishness put a dead-lock upon nearly everything that an enlightened view of the interests of all would have counselled to be done. In these circumstances, to succeed in foreign trade must have required no small amount of skill and policy, as well as means, because in addition to all the natural difficulties, there were bad laws to be evaded or overcome, or privileges and exemptions to be purchased from corrupt statesmen. There were also in those days sumptuary laws for preventing the people from injuring themselves by too expensive habits. They are understood to have not been very effectual for their avowed purpose; but they now serve a good end in revealing to us the nature of the business of the mercer in the times to which they refer. We find, for example, in 1581, when the country was but a few years emerged from a calamitous civil war, that even people of what was called 'mean estate' were addicted to 'the wearing of costly cleithing, of silks of all sorts, laine, cambric, fringes, and passments of gold, silver, and silk, and woollen claith, made and brocht from foreign countries.' Hence, it was stated, the prices of these articles had grown to such a height 'as is not longer able to be sustained without the great skaith and inconvenience of the commonweal'—that is to say, gentles were of opinion that they would get such articles much cheaper, if there were no other customers for them. The general inclination for foreign finery was held all the more indefensible, seeing that 'God has granted to this realm sufficient commodities for claithing of the inhabitants thereof within the self, gif the people were vertuously employed in working of the same at hame.'

Another such act in 1621 ordained that no persons but those of the nobility, and others possessing six thousand merks of free yearly rent, should wear 'any clothing of gold or silver cloth, or any gold or silver lace upon their apparel;' neither should they use 'velvet, sattin, or other stuffs of silk.' Even those who were privileged by wealth to wear these articles, were forbidden to have embroidery, lace, or passments upon their clothes, 'except only a plain welting lace of silk upon the seams or borders.' They were also to observe that 'the said apparel of silk be no ways cut out upon other stuffs of silk, except upon a single taffeta.' By the same act, it was enjoined that no person of whatsoever degree, except those privileged as above, should have 'pearling or ribboning upon their ruffs, sarks, napkins, and socks;' and any pearling or ribboning so worn was to be 'of those made within the kingdom of Scotland,' under a high penalty. So, also, castor-hats, feathers for the head, and gold chains with pearls or stones, were forbidden for all except the privileged classes; and servants were restricted to home-made fustian, canvas, and other stuffs, and husbandmen to the common gray, blue, and *self-black* cloth of the country. By *self-black* I presume is meant cloth made of the wool of black sheep in its natural state. These plain and homely kinds of cloth were woven by the village websters out of yarn which the housewives and their maidens had spun by the winter fireside when there was no more pressing work to do. Such cloths, so made,

22

continued in use amongst simple rustic people down to the close of the last century, and partially even a little later. I believe they have now entirely disappeared.

Notwithstanding all impediments from bad and simply officious legislation, we can see that the first third of the seventeenth century was a time of mercantile prosperity and progress in Scotland generally, and in Edinburgh in particular. The country was at peace; the laws were tolerably well executed; and as yet the religious troubles of the century had not begun. There was a general disposition, encouraged by the king, to see the useful arts cultivated in our country; and several were actually now established for the first time. For example, it was now that leather was first made of good quality in Scotland, the improved art being introduced by workmen from England. The manufacture of glass was set up in 1610 at Wemyss in Fife, by the ancestor of the Earls of Kinnoul, and met with tolerable success. Paper and a superior kind of cloth were attempted, but unsuccessfully. A great grudge being entertained regarding the large sums annually sent to Flanders for soap, there was much interest excited by an effort made at Leith, in 1619, to manufacture that useful article. The enterpriser was Mr Nathaniel Udwart, son of the Nicol Udwart who had entertained King James in his house in Niddry's Wynd. As an encouragement, he asked a privilege excluding the foreign article for a number of years, and the Privy Council took much pains to ascertain if this could be done without prejudice to the public. Pages after pages of their records are filled with deliberations on the subject, marginally marked with the words, 'Anent the Sape,' or 'Mr Nathaniel his sape;' and finally, he obtained the desired privilege under certain conditions. In this matter, however, flesh and blood could not endure the false political economy. Mr Nathaniel's soap was pronounced to be of unsatisfactory quality; and it was shewn to be better for the people in such distant provinces as Dumfries, to import their soap from Flanders, than to transport it from Leith by land-carriage. The native soap-factory appears, therefore, to have had a considerable struggle at first. Afterwards, it was more successfully carried on, along with the making of potasses, by Patrick Maule, the ancestor of the Lords Panmure; for here is another of our wealthy noble families who were beholden to trade for some part of their fortunes. We really must not be too hard upon our ancestors for the false commercial maxims by which they made their own interests so much of a difficulty to themselves, for we ought to remember how recently we have shaken off some of these very maxims, and how greatly foreign nations yet suffer from them. I daresay you will all hear, with something like a smile, that the proceedings of King James in 1598, regarding the poultrymen of Edinburgh, who tried to evade an edict for maximum prices, by selling their poultry in secret to people who would give better prices, were precisely imitated by the present Emperor of France in 1856, with respect to the butchers of Paris.

And in what, it will be asked, did the external commerce of Scotland at this time consist? First, then, was the exporting of wool, woollen and linen yarn, hides, tallow, butter, oil, and barrelled flesh, salmon, and herrings, also plaiden stuff and stockings, to the Low Countries. This was a trade exclusively confined by strict regulation to the port of Campvere, where, for many years past, there had been established a corporation of Scottish merchants, under a chief called the *Conservator*. It was a body entirely independent of the local authorities, as well of their High Mightinesses of the Netherlands; for the Conservator, with a council of six, or at least four, was entitled to adjudge in every case connected with Scottish merchants or merchandise. The Scottish merchants had a street and a quay to themselves, and a minister of their own choice, to whom the native mayor paid a salary of nine hundred guilders per annum. Second, there was a considerable trade with Poland, the goods being introduced by Scottish merchants residing at Dantzig, while the country itself was said to swarm with pedlers of our nation, by whom, I presume, the merchandise was diffused. Our townsman, Mr W. F. Skene, tells me that he lately found at Dantzig abundant records of the Scotch merchandise formerly carried on there. The imports were wool and coarse cloths; the exports, corn, tar, and wine—whence the latter was brought to Dantzig does not appear, but it might be from some countries far to the south, for through the Vistula there were communications between this Hanseatic town and districts far removed in that direction. Next, we must advert to a constant import of wine from France, probably for the most part in exchange for salmon and herrings. Finally, Scotland kept a considerable quantity of shipping in the employment of France, Spain, and even Italy and Barbary. The zealous clergy, in 1592, made an effort to stop this and every other kind of intercourse of their countrymen with Spain, from an apprehension, already adverted to, that they might thus be drawn back to Romanism; but here feelings of mercantile interest were too much for even clerical zeal, and the attempt failed miserably. The trade with France was threatened in a more serious manner in 1615, when, in consequence of an edict against the importation of goods into England in other than English vessels, the French king ordered that no goods should be imported from Britain into France in other than French vessels. A Scotch bark then lading at a French port was actually stopped, and ordered to go away empty. It was a most serious affair for Scotland; but the national ingenuity prevailed. France was reminded of the ancient alliance of King Alpin of Scotland with Charlemagne—a fable, but as good as a truth, since it was universally believed—also of the more palpable fact that Scotland, as apart from England, had issued no edict against French vessels. The rule was therefore relaxed in favour of Scottish ships. One of the standing troubles of this Scotch trade lay in the piratical habits of Algiers. Every now and then a piteous tale came home to Edinburgh of some little vessel, belonging to Dundee, or Leith, or Borrowstounness, caught by these rovers, and the crew all lying chained in dungeons, on the coast of Africa, fed with only bread and water. And then there would be a kindly collection of half-pence at the kirk-doors for the unfortunates, who generally were relieved by these means, though sometimes not till they had endured for a year or two their miserable captivity.

When troubles began to arise in consequence of the efforts of the kings James and Charles to introduce episcopalian arrangements and ceremonies, there were several eminent merchants of Edinburgh who stood conspicuously forward against these innovations. We hear much at that time of William Rig or Ridge, of Athernie in Fife, and of John Mean, both merchants in Edinburgh, very pious men, who, with John Hamilton, an apothecary, were banished to distant towns because they would not agree to accept the communion kneeling. Rig was both rich and liberal, insomuch that he is stated to have been in the custom of distributing annually upwards of eight thousand merks (equal to £444 sterling) for pious and charitable purposes. John Mean, whose wife is believed to have been the person who threw the stool at the bishop's head in St Giles's, at the reading of the famous *Service-book*, was at one time post-master of Edinburgh, that important institution having been set up in 1635: the revenue, in his time, was about four hundred a year. Another, and still more remarkable Edinburgh merchant, noted as a friend of the Presbyterian cause, was William Dick, ancestor of our neighbour Sir William Cunningham Dick of Prestonfield. Coming of Orkney people, one of his first adventures was the farming of the crown-rents of that district at three thousand pounds sterling. He established an active trade with the Baltic and the Mediterranean, and made a profitable business of negotiating bills of exchange with Holland. He had ships on every sea, and could ride on his own lands from North Berwick to near Linlithgow. His wealth, centering in a warehouse in the Luckenbooths, on the site of that now occupied by John Clapperton & Co., is estimated to have finally reached the astonishing sum of two hundred thousand pounds sterling; though I must own to some incredulity on the subject. That it was, however, very great, fully appears from the effects of it which appear in history. Sir William, having been induced to accept the provostship of the city in the year 1638, was easily led by his own religious prepossessions to become a sort of voluntary exchequer for the friends of the national covenant, then mustering a resistance to the Service-book and the bishops. King Charles could not have been faced at Dunse Law but for William Dick's cornucopia of dollars. From the same fund came the expenses for the king's visit to Edinburgh in 1641. When the Scottish parliament in the same year mustered ten thousand men to go to Ireland and suppress the rebel Catholics, the little army could not have marched without the meal which Sir William Dick furnished. His national loans afterwards extended to transactions in which the credit of the English parliament was concerned; and here ruin overtook him. The time came when such loans were not recognised, or at least met with but slight reverence; and this Scottish Crœsus—a national creditor to the extent of sixty-four thousand pounds—actually spent his last days in a jail at Westminster, under something like a want of the common necessaries of life.

While it appears that so many noted merchants stood up for the popular cause, that of royalty was espoused by at least one eminent trader, namely, Sir William Gray of Pittendrum, a cadet of the noble house of Gray, and direct ancestor of the present lord. Sir William, whose house, with his arms and initials, and the date 1622, may still be seen in Lady Stair's Close, Lawnmarket, is said to have conducted foreign trade upon a large scale, considering the times, and he became, for his age, extremely rich. For corresponding with the Marquis of Montrose, a fine of a hundred thousand merks was imposed upon him, and he actually paid thirty-five thousand, being nearly two thousand pounds sterling. When one of his sons married the Mistress of Gray, Sir William gave him the handsome endowment of 232,000 merks. Sir William Dick and Sir William Gray are perhaps the first commercial men of our city who reached the character of merchant-princes.

A little later than these men was James Stuart, a historical personage of even greater celebrity, and the more worthy of note on the present occasion, in as far as he made a movement to the formation of a Merchants' Company in Edinburgh so early as 1658. Born of the family of the Stuarts of Allanton in Lanarkshire, he was brought up in a merchant's shop in Edinburgh, and in due time became a flourishing merchant himself. His importance in this capacity, his active talents and address, made him a conspicuous actor on the popular side in the affairs of Scotland during the years of the civil war. Family tradition represents him as the person who brought to the Covenanters in Edinburgh that doubtful promise of sympathy and assistance from the English patriots, which is adverted to in all the histories of the period. It is stated that he was in London on business, when Lord Saville, hearing of him as a leading citizen of Edinburgh, and a man of talent and spirit, already noted amongst those who were contemplating a resistance to the king, sent for him, and after some conversation, bade him be of good cheer, for his countrymen would not be left to fight the battle single-handed. Whatever truth there is in this, James Stuart afterwards became a most distinguished public person. He was provost of Edinburgh in the trying time when it was invested, and at length taken possession of, by the troops of Cromwell. He survived the Restoration, and was a sufferer under Charles II.'s rule, but nevertheless left considerable realised wealth to his descendants, the Stuarts baronets of Coltness. His son was lord advocate under King William and Queen Anne; and the grandson of that personage wrote the first systematic work on political economy which appeared in this country.

The unsuccessful efforts made by Scotland first to extend presbytery into England under the Solemn League and Covenant, and next to save the old monarchy from the English sectaries and republicans, left it exhausted and bleeding under the heel of Cromwell. We should vainly, amidst our present peace and comfort, attempt to form an idea of the utter bankruptcy of our country during the eight or nine years when it was kept down by eight thousand

English soldiers, whom it was obliged to pay by a monthly cess for their oppression. Glasgow had then but twelve vessels, mostly under a hundred tons each; the customs of Leith, which have in our times touched six hundred thousand pounds, were then only £2335. We wade through year after year of the domestic annals of the country at this time, and hear of not one prosperous merchant, not one attempt at an enlarged system of industry, no new invention or project, nor even of the continuation of any of those manufactures which had been introduced during the two preceding reigns. Religious and political controversy, working itself out in violence fatal to all real progress, had blighted the whole pith and capacity of the country.

After the Restoration, things were for a long time not much better, for still unfortunately the bitterness of religious conflict was kept up. A Royal Fishery Company, with a capital of £25,000 sterling, was started, as a rival to the Dutch; but it did not prosper greatly. It had various privileges; and we rather hear of these proving a detriment to private enterprise, than of any distinct good done by the company itself. Amongst the most notable uses for shipping in the reign of the restored Stuart, were some of a melancholy character—privateering against the Dutch during the two shameful wars carried on against Holland, and the transporting of poor people to Barbadoes, and of discontented west-country Presbyterians to the American colonies. The former kind of work is said to have enriched two merchants named Baird, whose descendants have since figured among the Scottish gentry. But all such work was of small advantage to the country at large, as everything is, indeed, except that which gives real labour and its products. Here and there was a speculator like Sir Robert Mylne of Barnton, who made a little fortune by farming the entire national revenue at ninety thousand pounds, and ultimately lost it again, as he well might in that age without any necessary connection of the event with the fact of his having handed the Covenant to the hangman when it was publicly burnt after the Restoration. In this age, too, there was at least one able and successful merchant in our city, namely, Sir James Dick of Prestonfield, a grandson of the Rothschild of the Covenant. In him the fortunes of the family were in some measure restored. As provost of Edinburgh, he acquired the friendship of the Duke of York, when he lived at Holyrood, and used to be consulted by him about means of promoting the prosperity of the country. George Watson, the founder of our hospital, was originally head-clerk or accountant to Dick, at a salary of £16, 13s. 4d. Rather unexpectedly, I am informed that a branch of Sir James's business has continued to be kept up, and after some changes of situation, now appears under the firm of Craig Brothers, in the South Bridge. There was, however, in this reign, little more than a blind groping towards mercantile enterprise. The contemplation of English prosperity had created a spirit of emulation. Men of enlarged minds were sadly sensible of the national poverty. There was a general sense of uneasiness under the knowledge that perhaps as much as *twenty thousand a year* went out of this poor country into fat and comfortable England, to buy superfine cloth and other fineries for the upper classes. England, too, it was observed, had those colonies on the other side of the Atlantic, not one of whom could buy a hat, or a coat, or a sheet of glass, from anybody but an Englishman, while Scotland had no such outlets for manufactures, even if the manufactures existed. There was, it appears, in Scotland, the shrewd head and the willing hand; but how to start, how to get capital, skill, and experience—how, in short, to realise the ambitious views she was beginning to cherish!

Restricted as merchandise was in the reign of King William, we then find a general acknowledgment of the importance of the mercantile class in Edinburgh, in the practice of receiving the Lord Provost of the city as a member of the Privy Council, which was substantially the government of the country. These provosts, too, were generally knighted. Amongst them we find Sir John Hall, ancestor of the baronets of Dunglass, and of the late ingenious writer, Captain Basil Hall. Sir William Binning and

Sir Thomas Kennedy, who had been provosts in the late Stuart reigns, continued in that of King William to be engaged in large undertakings, such as government contracts and farmings of customs. So, also, was an eminent member of our Company, Bailie Alexander Brand, who finally acquired the honour of knighthood. We find Brand, for instance, along with Binning and Kennedy, engaging to import five thousand stand of arms for the state, at one pound sterling each, and getting into trouble from making public in a law-court that he contemplated a *donative* of two hundred and fifty guineas, with other articles, to some of the principal state-officers with whom the bargain had been made. A certain Sir Robert Dickson, who, with Binning and Kennedy, farmed the customs and foreign excise for five years from 1693, at twenty thousand three hundred pounds a year, got into a worse scrape still with the state-officers; for, in squaring accounts, he found upwards of two thousand pounds unexpectedly on the debit side, for wines given as gratuities to those nobles, and, seeking the king's protection from this oppression, he found himself liable to a charge, under an old statute, against murmuring at judges, and was glad to buy himself off by craving pardon on his knees. The gratuities, in the latter case, were declared to be according to use and wont; if so, it seems hard that Brand should have been harassed for announcing a compliance with the custom in the other case; but, of course, *quietness* is everything in these matters.

It was in this reign that the bearing of the national mind towards commerce first found effectual gratification. A company, headed by John Holland, a London merchant, started in 1695 the Bank of Scotland, the first institution of the kind in the country. Its paid-up capital was at first no more than ten thousand pounds. It tried branches at Aberdeen, Dundee, and Glasgow; but they did not succeed, or were not found to be wanted, and the money was all brought home again on horses' backs. Under the prompting and guidance of an ingenious native, William Paterson, the African Company was formed in the ensuing year, with about a quarter of a million of paid-up capital, and the design of planting a great entrepôt for the commerce of the world on the Isthmus of Darien. As is well known, this company, through English jealousy, proved a disastrous failure. It was a sore blow for a poor country to suffer at the very opening of a mercantile career, and it was long before our people forgot it, or overcame its effects. When the Union, however, happily settled that English exclusivism was no longer exclusive for Scotland—when Scotland was so far allowed to have that fair-play for her industry which we are now seeking to establish as the right of all, as it is for the good of all—then did her enterprise find safer channels and a more fitting reward. Owing, indeed, to the lack of capital and other causes, the progress was for a long time rather slow, and especially on our side of the island. As a proof of this, take the contrast between the shipping of Leith in 1692—twenty-nine vessels of an average of fifty-nine tons (the value £7100)—and that of 1740, when it exhibited forty-seven vessels of an average of only fifty-six tons, and not one above 180. The increase of the next twelve years to sixty-eight vessels, of an average of 102 tons—several being as high as 300, and one of 350 tons—shews a great acceleration of progress after the first difficulties were got over. In 1844, there belonged to Leith 210 vessels of an aggregate of 25,427 tons, or an average of 121 tons. On the west side of the island, owing to the development of the American colonies, the progress was greater; and yet it was not till eleven years after the Union that Glasgow sent her first ship across the Atlantic. The smallness of all mercantile matters there at first is most remarkable. It is alleged that four young men, with ten thousand pounds amongst them, commenced the mercantile glory of our western capital. And one cannot without a smile read, in the diary of serious Mr Wodrow, under 1709, of Glasgow losing no less than ten thousand pounds by the capture of a fleet going to Holland. 'I am sure,' he says, 'the Lord is remarkably frowning upon our trade in more respects than one, since it was put in place of our religion, in the late alteration of our constitution.' Leaving these more general matters, I must devote the remainder of my brief space to the history of the Merchant Company of Edinburgh.

It was amidst some of the most distressing things in our national history—hangings of the poor 'hill-folk' in the Grassmarket, trying of the patriot Argyle for taking the test with an explanation, and so forth—that this Company came into being. Its nativity was further heralded by sundry other things of a troublous kind, more immediately affecting merchandise and its practitioners.

The superior woollen cloth which was woven in England so early as the reign of Henry VIII., made its way into Scotland before the end of the sixteenth century; but it was very grudgingly looked upon by our native economists. The 'hame-bringing of English claith' was denounced in an act of 1597 as an unprofitable trade, 'the same claith having only for the maist part an outward show, wanting that substance and strength whilk ofttimes it appears to have,' and being, moreover, the chief cause of the 'transporting of all gold and silver furth of this realm, and, consequently, of the present dearth of the cunyie.' Soon after this, seven Flemings were brought to Edinburgh, to instruct the people how to make *seys* and broadcloth at home, and to save this pernicious outflow of coin into England; but there were many impediments in the way. We do not hear that the seven

Flemings were ever fairly set to work. In 1620, a second attempt of the same kind was made with four Fleming cloth-makers, in a place on the outskirts of the city called Paul's Work; but the days were still evil. The first really energetic or hopeful effort at a woollen-cloth manufacture amongst us was not made till the year 1681, when a work of that kind was set up at Newmills, near Haddington, under the care of an Englishman named Stanfield, and with several English workmen to instruct the natives. As what was thought a needful encouragement to this and other enterprises for the production of articles of attire within the country, and so saving money from being sent out of it, an act of parliament was passed, forbidding the importation of all kinds of cloth of wool or lint, all silk goods, and, generally, articles of personal finery; also the exporting of any linen or woollen yarn, or of any coarse cloth. It was called an act for encouraging trade and manufactures; but while it could not very readily bring manufactures into being, it was in reality calculated to extinguish no small amount of trade. Very amusingly, too, the act recites that these arrangements were arrived at by the Privy Council 'after long and serious deliberation, and advice of the most judicious and knowing merchants of the kingdom.' It is scarce conceivable to us how such an act came to be passed, seeing that it forbade the use of foreign articles before any corresponding ones were made at home; before even the machinery for making them was set up or existed; but the truth is, the governments of those days had much greater dependence upon the use of force than we have—force to make people like bishops or give up popery—force to direct what they were to eat, and what they were to wear. And with all this dependence on force, no means of really enforcing anything: at least, we never hear of any such enactments in those days, but we soon after hear of their being everywhere broken through and disregarded. For my part, I feel at a loss to understand the drift of the government on this occasion, for, little more than two months after a parliamentary prohibition of foreign cloth, we find the king giving the *Company of the Merchants of Edinburgh* their Patent, describing them as *invectores et panni tam rasi quam villosi*, importers of both fine and coarse cloth. Probably it was expected that they would almost instantly cease to be so, and remain only liable to the rest of the description given to them of *vendors of wearing stuffs*. If so, the hope was a bootless one, for, notwithstanding sundry burnings of the forbidden foreign stuffs on the streets of Edinburgh, no manufacture either of fine woollen cloth, or of silks, or fine linen, took hearty root in our country for many years thereafter. Most likely, the act fell speedily into contempt as impracticable.

It was on the 1st of December 1681 that eighty-two merchants of Edinburgh, so called, but in truth specially concerned in the business of cloth or clothing alone, met the magistrates in the High Council-house, to hear read the royal letters-patent, erecting them into a company or society for the promotion of commerce and sundry other useful purposes. Each member was to pay at entry three pounds Scots—that is, ten shillings sterling—and six shillings Scots, or an English sixpence, yearly, while in trade, for the purpose of constituting a fund for decayed members and their widows and children. It will be observed that these were very moderate contributions, even for the reign of Charles II.; but the tradition of the Company is, that its whole scheme was at first of a humble nature. The constituent members adopted as their symbol a *Stock of Broom*—a modest shrub, but with a great tendency to increase. As such they regarded their society and plan of charity; and ever since, 'the Stock of Broom' has been the first toast at all the convivial meetings of the Company. I regret to remark, that, while such laudable views and ideas prevailed amongst our predecessors, the universal taint of exclusiveness had also an ascendency over them. It was ruled in their very constitution, that none who had not entered their Company should be permitted to practise merchandise in the city. And they were entitled to poind goods which were exposed to sale in contravention of their bye-laws.

One of the Company's first proceedings was to ask the Dean of Edinburgh (Very Reverend William Annand) to compose a prayer to be said by the clerk at all their meetings. It was as follows: 'Almighty and eternal God, we thy servants now assembled, implore, according to thy gracious promises, the pardon of all our offences, and thy holy spirit to deliver us from falling into the snares of sin and Satan. Keep us, O Lord, in peace, unity, brotherly love, and concord, by removing pride, prejudice, passion, covetousness, and whatever may offend thy gracious majesty. Bless our king and all the royal family, the magistrates, and all the incorporations of this city, the Masters and all the members of this society, that we may have fellowship with thee. The sea is thine, and thy hands formed the dry land: prosper us in our present undertaking with the fruits of both; above all, with the fruits of thy holy Spirit, through Jesus Christ our Lord.' It was thought proper to make some requital to the dean for this service; but it seems to have been rather long before the Stock of Broom spread sufficiently to allow of this being done. It was not till August 1686 that the Company ordained Hugh Blair, one of their number, to furnish the reverend gentleman with 'six ells fine black cloth for a gown,' for which 'the said Hugh Blair is to have from the Company twenty shillings sterling the ell, *if it be paid within twelve months*; but if it happen to be any longer resting, the price is to be augmented at the discretion of the Company conform to the time.' On the 9th of January 1688 the Company realised £36, 13s. Scots, or rather more than three pounds sterling, by poindings of certain small quantities of fustian, mohair, and serge, which had been exposed in the market contrary to law; and, now believing themselves to be in a good way, they ordered that Hugh Blair be paid for the dean's gown out of the first and readiest of the treasurer's intromissions, but still to be allowed interest till payment was actually made. We may presume that Blair was paid not long after this, for, in the ensuing September, the twelve pounds Scots realised from the fustian was ordered to be given to James Tait, an indigent member of the Company. It may be remarked that Hugh Blair was a grandson of Robert Blair, one of the Covenanting ministers who have reached a historical fame, and he was at the same time grandfather to his namesake the admired minister of the High Kirk, and author of the *Sermons* and *Lectures on Belles-Lettres*. Hugh was Master of the Company in the year 1692. It may also be worth while to recall that Dean Annand was the clergyman officially appointed to attend the unfortunate Earl of Argyle on the scaffold. He was a man of considerable learning, and, as we learn from his communications with Argyle, a hearty opponent of popery.

One of the Company's earliest movements of any importance was the acquiring of a hall; but I regret to say this was not, as might be supposed, a movement of a purely dignified nature—the great object was to get a place of their own, in which they could deposit the goods taken from unfreemen, it having been found hitherto, that such goods taken to private houses were often disposed of clandestinely: in short, the Company got little good of them. In 1691, the Master, Bailie Robert Blackwood, intimated that there was a suitable house to be had in the Cowgate—namely, a large lodging belonging to Viscount Oxenford, and the price would be about twelve thousand merks, or six hundred and seventy pounds sterling. A subscription was immediately entered into to defray the cost, and the house was purchased. It was a large quadrangular building, surrounding a court-yard, and had been the residence of the celebrated lawyer of a hundred years before, who finally became the first Earl of Haddington—popularly called, from his locality, *Tam o' the Cowgate*. Even now, the widow of the cavalier Sir Thomas Dalyell of Binns, and one or two other persons of quality, had lodgment in some of its apartments. There was one large room which was to be devoted to the purposes of a hall; but it was sadly out of order. Presently comes forward a liberal member of the Company, Bailie Alexander Brand, who had some time before established a manufactory of what was called *Spanish leather*, for the ornamenting of rooms—namely, skins stamped with gold. It was a pretty style of hangings, once in great favour in Scotland; a few examples may still be seen in old country-houses; one I remember in the house of Gartsherrie in Lanarkshire. The bailie undertook to hang the hall in this manner, and only charge what was due over and above his own contribution of a hundred and fifty pounds Scots. Ten years afterwards, when accounts came to be settled with the then Sir Alexander Brand—for it will be observed prompt settlements were by no means among the commercial virtues of our predecessors—it appeared that a hundred and nineteen skins of gold leather, with a black ground, had been used, at a total expense of two hundred and fifty-three pounds Scots, including the manufacturer's contribution. There was also much concernment about a piece of waste ground behind; but the happy thought occurred of converting it into a bowling-green, for the use of the members in the first place, and the public in the second. Many years after, we find Allan Ramsay making joyous Horatian allusions to this place of recreation, telling us that now, in winter, douce folk were no longer seen wysing ajee the biassed bowls on Tamson's Green (Thomson being a subsequent tenant). It is not unworthy of notice that, from the low state of the arts in Scotland, the bowls required for this green had to be brought from abroad. It is gravely reported to the Company on the 6th of March 1693, that the bowls are 'upon the sea homeward.' Ten pair cost £6, 4s. 3d. Scots. It is scarcely necessary to add that the Company's connection with the Cowgate was dissolved long ago, and even the house has for thirty years ceased to exist, having been taken down to make way for George the Fourth's Bridge. The only remaining memorial of the Company at that spot is to be found in the name, Merchant Street, applied to a half-extinguished line of buildings behind the Cowgate, and our title to the ground-rents of that part of the city.

By and by, the Company became engaged in matters more amiable than the seizing of goods of unfreemen. Wealthy members died, leaving *mortifications* (in the happy Scottish sense) to the Company, for the succour of decayed brethren. It is remarkable that, on the first such occasion, in 1693, when three thousand five hundred pounds, accruing from a legacy left by Patrick Aikenhead, a Scotch merchant at Dantzig, for pious uses in Edinburgh, came into possession of the Merchant Company, they had not a decayed member requiring the benefit. Not long after the last date, the Company became engaged in the erection of a hospital for the nurture and education of the female children of their less prosperous members. Though originated by a certain Mrs Hare, widow of an Edinburgh apothecary, but a scion of the noble house of Marr, the principal labour and expense attending this foundation fell upon the Merchant Company of Edinburgh. Their zeal in the affair is amply shewn in their books, where the entries of contributions for 'the Lasses' are for some years incessant. Twenty-eight years later, when George Watson died, leaving no less than twelve thousand pounds sterling for the benefit of children of the other sex, the Merchant Company came to have the management of a second foundation of the same kind. I believe its administration in both hospitals has, generally speaking, been unexceptionable. It is, however, worthy of observation, that the Company itself has never supplied a sufficiency of children requiring the benefits. It has conducted these institutions to a considerable extent on the principle of *Vos non vobis*.

It is foreign to my purpose to trace the history of Edinburgh merchants and merchandise during the time following upon the Union, when the national industry and enterprise, being allowed a fair field, were producing those results of wealth and civilisation which we now see smiling around us. I may remark, however, that the first two Georges were inurned before the merchants of this or any other British city had ceased in any degree to depend on prohibitions of this and that, and exclusive rights to deal and be dealt with. The introduction of Indian damasks, padasoys, and taffetas was, so lately as 1730, spoken of by our Merchant Company as 'destructive.' In England, 'Bury in woollen if you have any bowels for your country,' was a general feeling, and, indeed, a matter of law. The late Bailie Robert Johnston once shewed me a curious document, drawn up and extensively signed by the Edinburgh mercers and drapers, about the year 1760, covenanting that henceforth they would wholly cease to traffic with that generation of men called 'English riders.' So long is it before an enlightened sense of interests, even among a shrewd and tolerably well-educated people, supersedes the first stringent emotions of human selfishness. How different the spirit of the Merchant Company, and its offshoot the Chamber of Commerce, has been in recent times, patronising and promoting every liberal measure, need not be dwelt upon. Another particular of the last century may be adverted to—namely, that there continued to be a very great infusion among our merchants of what may be called an aristocratic element. On this subject I am aided by the recollections of the late venerable clerk of the Company, Mr James Jollie, extending nearly a century back from the present time. To take the leading firms among the silk-mercers. Of John Hope and Company, the said John Hope was a younger son of Hope of Rankeillour in Fife. Of Stewart and Lindsay, the former was the son of Charles Stewart of Ballechen, and the latter a younger son of Lindsay of Wormiston. Among the leading drapers: in the firm of Lindsay and Douglas, the former was a younger son of Lindsay of Eaglescairney, and the latter of

Douglas of Garvaldfoot. Of Dundas, Inglis, and Callander, the first was son to Dundas of Fingask in Stirlingshire, the family from which the Earl of Zetland and Baron Amesbury are descended; the second was a younger son of Sir John Inglis of Cramond, and succeeded to that baronetage, which, it may be remarked, took its rise in an Edinburgh merchant of the seventeenth century. Another eminent cloth-dealing firm, Hamilton and Dalrymple, comprehended John Dalrymple, a younger brother of the well-known Lord Hailes, and a great grandson of the first Lord Stair: he was at one time Master of the Merchant Company. In a fourth firm, Stewart, Wallace, and Stoddart, the leading partner was a son of Stewart of Dunearn. The leading wine-merchants and bankers of those days were also men of family; but this, of course, is the less worthy of remark, as it continues in some degree to be the case at the present day.

That so many landed families amongst us have descended from Edinburgh merchants is no singular fact, for trade efflorescing into nobility is an old phenomenon in the south. There we have a Duke of Leeds descended from the apprentice of Sir William Hewit the goldsmith; the Wentworth Fitzwilliams, from a worthy London merchant knighted by Henry VIII. From the nautical adventurer Phipps, of the time of Charles II., come the Earls of Mulgrave. Cornwallis is from a London merchant; Coventry, from a mercer; Radnor, from a silk-manufacturer; Warwick, from a wool-stapler; Pomfret, from a Calais merchant. Essex, Dartmouth, Craven, Tankerville, Darnley, Cowper, and Romney, have all had a similar origin. More recently ennobled families—the Dacres, the Dormers, the Dudley Wards, the Hills, the Caringtons, have in like manner taken their rise from successful trade. It is an origin surely as honourable as dexterous courtiership, gifts of church-lands, or mediæval robbery and plunder.

On a retrospect of the whole subject, one must see that, notwithstanding so many of our merchants of old being gentlefolks, there is a great improvement in many respects amongst the class. Our predecessors had not merely to contend with the narrow resources of the country, and with the want of a thousand conveniences for the transport of goods by sea and land, which have since come into existence, but, worst of all, they had to struggle with the dictates of their own ignorance. Nearly all the principles which they advanced and sought to realise in legislation, as for the encouragement of trade and manufactures, were false, and could only operate for the repression of the industrial energies of the community, and, by consequence, for the keeping up of poverty in the land. It is a strange thing to say, but it is true, that breakers of laws have in a great measure been the means of bringing about a sounder policy. We have happily got above the greater part of these errors, and daily reap the natural advantages of our superior light; and yet, as a part of the British community, I think we ought to feel modest about the faults of our ancestors, since it is undeniable that the commercial world is still far from having attained the summit of perfection. It has faults, too, which are almost peculiar to our own age. The advance by banks of large sums of deposited money to reckless traders destitute of capital of their own, and who only hope for some trump to turn up in their favour before ruin overtakes them, is a mercantile error which our ancestors never dreamed of. So, also, those consequent disastrous crises of trade, of which we have just seen an example sweep over the industrial world, were unknown to our forefathers. The present Company may, however, be gratified in reflecting that from these errors the old banking companies of Edinburgh have been comparatively free. The five or six great banks of old standing amongst us not only came out safe in the late crisis, but they were able to hold out help to some at a distance which were less fortunate. As a humble individual of this community, I must say I feel a pride in the old Edinburgh banks, as an exponent of business procedure amongst us. If we overlook only the brief civil war of 1745, when the grandfather of our present sheriff-clerk—being cashier to the Royal Bank—marched up in his tartans, pistols, and claymore, to deposit the bank's money in the castle, that it might be safe from his less scrupulous countrymen, and when the Bank of Scotland was but too happy to follow the example—there we see doors which have never for a day been closed for a hundred and forty-four years! I was going to have said a hundred and sixty-four years; but on looking into the history of the Bank of Scotland, I find there was a brief stoppage of cash-payments in 1704 occasioned by a malicious run, and another caused by the civil troubles of the year 1715. As it is, overlooking only the unavoidable cessation of business in the Forty-five, the doors of the 'Auld Bank' have been in the ordinary condition of those of the temple of Janus at Rome for a hundred and forty-four years. It cannot have been without consummate prudence that this glory has been achieved. During the late crisis, moreover, the number of failures in our city, including Leith, was comparatively small. It will be said, perhaps, that Edinburgh is not a city of much business—a saying against which I take leave to reclaim. It is, for one thing, the centre of monetary business for the kingdom. The life-assurance companies and societies of Scotland—hitherto, like our old banks, of untainted character—have, with but little exception, their headquarters here; and let us just passingly observe, three of these establishments in St Andrew Square enjoy an annual income of six hundred and fifty thousand pounds, and have the management of accumulated funds to the extent of five and a half millions.[2] When we further consider the legal business of Edinburgh, its agenting of property throughout the country, its large publishing establishments, its glass-works and foundries, its merchandise in wine and drysaltery, it is, even leaving Leith out of view, in reality very much a city of business. While, then, I acknowledge that we are still everywhere under more or less of commercial error, I think it may at the same time be allowable to describe the mercantile community of Edinburgh, as one in which experience has proved that a more than usually sound and prudent practice—with happy fruits—has the ascendant.

FOOTNOTES:

[1] For these interesting particulars, I am indebted to Joseph Robertson, Esq., Record Office, Edinburgh.

[2] The Scottish Widows' Fund, Scottish Equitable, and Scottish Provident Offices, are here alluded to. The entire annual income of the life-assurance offices of Scotland, chiefly centering in Edinburgh, is stated at £2,082,000, and the sum-total of their funds at £11,116,000.—*Letter of R. Christie, Esq., Accountant, Courant newspaper, Feb. 26, 1859.*